ERIC HUANG

Oh No They DIDN'T

PRESIDENTS

also Vice Presidents, First Ladies, and presidential pets!

CHESTER A. ARTHUR

ILLUSTRATED BY
SAM CALDWELL

words & pictures

© 2024 Quarto Publishing Group USA Inc.
Text © Eric Huang 2024
Illustrations © Sam Caldwell 2024

First published in 2024 by words & pictures,
an imprint of The Quarto Group.
100 Cummings Center,
Suite 265D Beverly,
MA 01915, USA.
T (978) 282-9590 F (978) 283-2742
www.quarto.com

Copyeditor: Nancy Dickmann
Project Editor: Alice Hobbs
Designer: Kathryn Davies
Art Director: Susi Martin
Associate Publisher: Holly Willsher

A CIP record for this book is available from the Library of Congress.

ISBN: 978-0-7112-9284-0

Manufactured in Guangdong, China TT042024

9 8 7 6 5 4 3 2 1

MIX
Paper | Supporting
responsible forestry
FSC® C016973
FSC
www.fsc.org

ERIC HUANG

Oh No They DIDN'T

JOHN F. KENNEDY

PRESIDENTS

FASCINATING FACTS YOU NEVER KNEW ABOUT U.S. PRESIDENTS!

ILLUSTRATED BY
SAM CALDWELL

words & pictures

CONTENTS

When did presidents stop wearing hats?

Did the president always live at the White House?

Do you know the responsibilities of the FLOTUS?

INTRODUCTION

The people who have served as president of the United States of America—or POTUS for short—are some of the most famous people on the planet. We've all grown up learning about the elected leaders who guided our country during wartime as well as through times of peace, prosperity, and change. But how much do we really know about the presidents?

Well, we all know that **President Abraham Lincoln** freed enslaved people by signing the Emancipation Proclamation. And how about the most famous presidential story of all? The one about our first president, **George Washington**, who chopped down a cherry tree as a boy. Washington and Lincoln really did both of these things. . . didn't they?

OH NO THEY DIDN'T!

READ ON to discover which of the **famous stories** about our presidents **never really happened.**

You'll find out how much of what you know about our country's elected leaders is **actually true.**

The truth is stranger than fiction.

Let's cut to the facts.

Rolling through history...

Along the way, you'll also meet many of the **veeps** (that's **vice presidents**, for those not in the know) and **FLOTUSes (aka First Ladies)** who served at their side.

THE WHITE HOUSE

The White House is one of the world's most recognizable homes. As soon as the Revolutionary War ended, it was built in our new country's capital, Washington, D.C., as a home for the president. . . wasn't it?

OH NO IT WASN'T!

When the United States first became independent, we didn't really have a capital. In the early days, Philadelphia, Baltimore, Princeton, Annapolis, and New York City all served as centers of government. **George Washington** picked the location for building a brand-new capital city, but he never lived there. He lived in New York or Philadelphia while the White House and the rest of Washington, D.C. were being built.

By 1800, the White House was finally finished, but George Washington had retired to Virginia in March 1797 and passed away by December 1799. His vice president, **John Adams**, was now our second president—but the first to live in the White House. Talk about the dream home that got away!

The White House was built from sandstone—a grayish, yellowish rock. According to a popular story, the building was painted white to cover up fire damage from the War of 1812. . . wasn't it?

Which color matches the curtains?

OH NO IT WASN'T!

The White House was always white. The outside walls were painted with a white-colored wash that protected the structure from the freezing D.C. winters. Think of it as a cozy, white coat in liquid form!

Most people called the new building the "President's House" or the "Executive Mansion." "White House" was a nickname, only used in newspapers. It only became the official name in 1901, on the orders of the 26th president **Theodore Roosevelt**.

BEING PRESIDENT

Not just anyone can become president of the United States of America. There are some rules in the United States Constitution—three of them, to be exact:

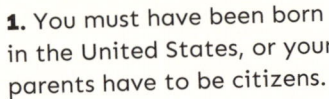

1. You must have been born in the United States, or your parents have to be citizens.

2. You must be at least 35 years old.

3. You have to have lived in the U.S. for 14 years.

So all of our presidents were 35 years or older, they were all born in the USA, and all grew up as American citizens. . . didn't they?

OH NO THEY DIDN'T!

John Adams

Andrew Jackson

George Washington

Seven presidents weren't born in the United States!

These seven didn't become American citizens until later in life. The list includes George Washington, the first president, who only became a citizen when he was 44 years old.

When the first seven presidents were born, what is now the United States of America was a collection of thirteen British colonies. People born in the colonies were subjects of the British Empire, not American citizens. The USA didn't exist yet!

These first seven presidents were **George Washington, John Adams, Thomas Jefferson, James Madison, James Monroe, John Quincy Adams, and Andrew Jackson,** and all of them were born in the British Empire. They became Americans when the United States of America declared its independence on July 4, 1776.

Over two million other colonists also became American citizens on the same day. Just imagine the lines to apply for a passport!

Thomas Jefferson

James Monroe

John Quincy Adams

James Madison

READY TO BE PRESIDENT

The role of president of the United States is one of the world's most important jobs. So all of them graduated from the best colleges and had high-profile jobs to prepare them for this demanding role... didn't they?

Our first president, **George Washington**, also didn't earn a college degree. He studied for a surveyor's license, instead. A surveyor is a specialist who measures and maps out land. It was an important job at a time when no one had map apps!

OH NO THEY DIDN'T!

Eleven presidents didn't earn a college degree. Andrew Johnson and Abraham Lincoln were two of them.

Andrew Johnson, the 17th president, didn't have any formal education at all—even as a boy! Johnson's family was very poor. He grew up in a two-room shack and had to drop out of school to work.

Abraham Lincoln, built a successful career as a lawyer despite never going to law school. He borrowed textbooks and studied on his own before qualifying as a lawyer in Illinois. If he *had* attended law school, he definitely would've been the teacher's pet!

Like Lincoln, many of our presidents had different jobs before they took office. The 40th president, **Ronald Reagan**, was a Hollywood star before going into politics. He appeared in more than 50 movies!

Jimmy Carter, who was president just before Reagan, served in the navy and then ran a peanut farm.

Before he became our 30th president, **Harry S. Truman** owned a haberdashery—a shop that sells men's clothing as well as buttons, zippers, thread, and fabric.

Bet you never knew that one of our presidents would be able to fix that hole in your sock!

★ THE PRESIDENTS ★

1

GEORGE WASHINGTON
(1789–1797)

The first president of the United States was George Washington. On his sixth birthday, Washington's dad gave him a hatchet. Young George ran outside, swinging the hatchet, and accidentally damaged a cherry tree in their garden. When his dad asked about the tree, George replied, "Father, I cannot tell a lie" and admitted to carelessly hurting the tree. . . didn't he?

OH NO HE DIDN'T!

This story was completely made up! In 1800, a writer named Mason Locke Weems wrote a biography of the first president, which became a bestseller. Weems made up the cherry tree story as a colorful way to show how honest George Washington was, even as a boy.

During George Washington's lifetime, modern toothpaste hadn't been invented yet, so many people lost their teeth from cavities. Many people cleaned their teeth by rubbing a rough cloth in their mouths. When George Washington's teeth fell out, he wore a set of false teeth made of wood. . . didn't he?

OH NO HE DIDN'T!

George Washington had several sets of false teeth throughout his life. They were never made of wood, which would fall apart quite quickly when wet.

Mooo!

Much more durable materials were used instead: the teeth of animals such horses, cows, and elephants—and sometimes even the teeth of people who were enslaved.

The dentures made from cow's teeth must've been quite the moo-thful!

15

JOHN ADAMS
(1797–1801)

2 **John Adams** was our country's first vice president before becoming the first president to live in the White House. Did you know that he wanted the president to be called "His Highness," thinking that a fancy title would give the POTUS more respect on the international stage?

Unfortunately, no one else liked the idea, so Adams was called "Mr. President" like all the rest.

Before Thomas Jefferson became president, he served as the minister for France and lived in Paris. When he returned to the United States, he introduced a popular European dessert called ice cream to America. . . didn't he?

OH NO HE DIDN'T!

Despite the story, ice cream had already reached America. But Jefferson is credited for the first written ice cream recipe in the country, one that was probably passed on to him by his French butler or by his cooking staff who had lived with him in France.

I scream, you scream. . .

3

THOMAS JEFFERSON
(1801–1809)

JAMES MADISON
[1809–1817]

4 **James Madison** was a passionate supporter of the Bill of Rights and is often called the "Father of the Constitution." But speaking of ice cream, it was Madison's wife Dolley who made America scream for ice cream, although her favorite flavor was oyster! It wasn't sweet—it was more of a creamy, frozen oyster soup.

James Monroe famously wrote the Monroe Doctrine. . . didn't he?

OH NO HE DIDN'T!

The Monroe Doctrine told the rest of the world that the United States was against the creation of new European colonies in the Americas. It's named after the president, even though it was mainly formulated by John Quincy Adams, who succeeded him as president.

5

JAMES MONROE
[1817–1825]

6 JOHN QUINCY ADAMS
[1825–1829]

7 ANDREW JACKSON
[1829–1837]

Andrew Jackson ended the War of 1812 with his celebrated victory at the Battle of New Orleans. . . didn't he?

OH NO HE DIDN'T!

John Quincy Adams was the son of the second president, John Adams. Did you know he was also the first president to speak against slavery?

The War of 1812 was a conflict between North America and the United Kingdom. While Jackson's victory at the Battle of New Orleans made him a hero, the battle didn't end the war. The treaty that ended the war was signed before the battle even started, but the news sadly didn't reach the troop in time.

Did you know that **Martin Van Buren** was the first president whose family didn't come from the British Isles? His ancestors were Dutch, and English was his second language. Even so, his birth after the Revolutionary war made him the first president born a U.S. citizen.

8 MARTIN VAN BUREN
[1837–1841]

WILLIAM HENRY HARRISON
[1841]

This poor man was only president for one month! He caught pneumonia at his inauguration and died from it. . . didn't he?

OH NO HE DIDN'T!

President Harrison did pass away from an illness, but the most likely cause is infection from contaminated drinking water at the White House. Its water came from a spring very close to a sewage plant.

Because John Tyler was vice president when Harrison died, he automatically became president. . . didn't he?

OH NO HE DIDN'T!

There were no rules about who would become president if the president died. But John Tyler quickly took the presidential oath, then moved into the White House. The rule that the vice president becomes president wouldn't become official for more than 100 years.

THIS WAY UP

JOHN TYLER
[1841–1845]

11

I'm done!

JAMES K. POLK
(1845–1849)

Did you know that **James K. Polk** made a promise that if elected, he would only serve one term? He vowed not to run for reelection—and kept his promise!

12

ZACHARY TAYLOR
(1849–1850)

Zachary Taylor was in office for just over a year before he ate an extra-large helping of cherries and ice cream and died. The dessert was poisoned. . . wasn't it?

OH NO IT WASN'T!

Rumors soon spread that he had been assassinated by arsenic in his ice cream! Scientists recently tested Taylor's hair and fingernails, but there wasn't enough arsenic to confirm the poisoning theory. It's more likely that contaminated water at the White House also caused Taylor's death. (Don't worry, the water at the White House is perfectly safe now!)

13

MILLARD FILLMORE
(1850–1853)

Did you know that **Fillmore** and his wife, Abigail, started the White House library? They brought their own books when they moved into the White House, and left them in the library when they moved out.

14

FRANKLIN PIERCE
(1853–1857)

Did you know that a thunderstorm changed **Franklin Pierce's** life? As a boy, he once played hooky from school.

When his father caught him, he took his naughty son back to school, but stopped the carriage halfway. Franklin's dad made him walk the rest of the way to school, several miles during a thunderstorm. The future POTUS learned a valuable lesson that day—to put in the hard work and never cut corners. And also maybe. . . always carry an umbrella!

15

JAMES BUCHANAN
(1857–1861)

HARRIET LANE

Did you know that **James Buchanan** is the only president who never married? He was president until about one month before the Civil War began. His sister Harriet Lane Johnston served as his first lady.

ABRAHAM LINCOLN
(1861–1865)

16

One of our most famous presidents, Abraham Lincoln freed enslaved people by signing the Emancipation Proclamation. . . didn't he?

OH NO HE DIDN'T!

The Emancipation Proclamation was an executive order signed by Abraham Lincoln in 1863. It ordered that all enslaved people within the states that seceded or broke away from the Union during the Civil War were now free. But there were still enslaved people in some states that hadn't left the Union, and these people weren't freed. Two years later, the 13th Amendment to the Constitution would officially end slavery. The last enslaved people to be freed were those in Galveston, Texas, on June 19, 1865. This date is celebrated today as the national holiday Juneteenth.

Abraham Lincoln is also known for the Gettysburg Address, a speech to dedicate a cemetery for soldiers who had fallen in the Battle of Gettysburg. He quickly wrote what became one of history's most memorable speeches on the back of an envelope while on a train. . . didn't he?

OH NO HE DIDN'T!

A tall order, even for Honest Abe.

Although the Gettysburg Address is only 272 words long, Lincoln spent weeks writing and rewriting it, consulting with many people before a final draft was ready. They must have gotten it right, because the legacy of this super-short speech has lasted for generations.

Did you know that Abraham Lincoln was the tallest president? He was 6 feet 4 inches tall—and that was without his top hat, which would've added an additional 7 to 8 inches! He was a true giant of a president.

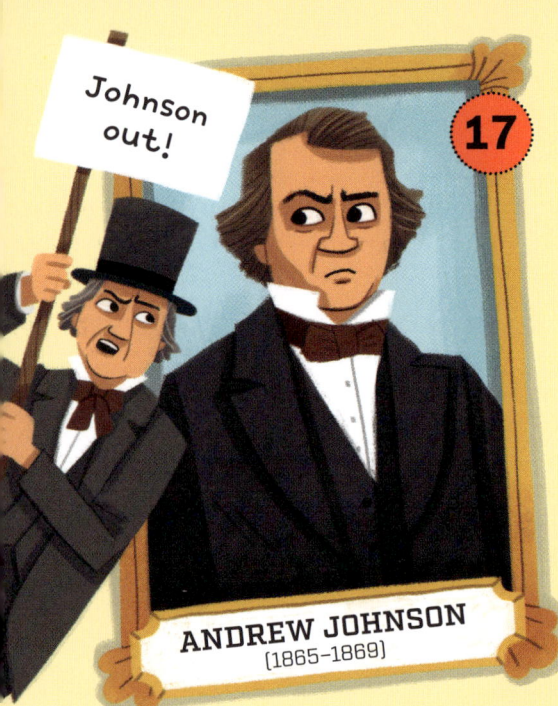

ANDREW JOHNSON
(1865–1869)

As president, Johnson was constantly at odds with many colleagues. In fact he was impeached by the House of Representatives and kicked out of office. . . wasn't he?

OH NO HE WASN'T!

Andrew Johnson was impeached, meaning he was accused of breaking the rules. But at the end of the trial, he was acquitted by one vote and kept his job.

President number 18 was a Civil War general named Ulysses S. Grant. . . wasn't he?

OH NO HE WASN'T!

ULYSSES S. GRANT
(1869–1877)

Ulysses S. Grant's real name was Hiram Ulysses Grant. Hiram was his grandfather's name, and Ulysses was picked out of a hat. So what does the "S" stand for? Well. . . nothing. It was a mistake! When Grant entered the military academy West Point, his name was written incorrectly as "Ulysses S. Grant," and it stuck.

19

RUTHERFORD B. HAYES
(1877–1881)

President Hayes is remembered for starting the White House Easter Egg Roll. This children's race takes place every Easter Monday. Contestants roll their eggs through the grass, using a spoon. This is one time when playing with your food is okay!

20

"But I am Garfield!?"

JAMES A. GARFIELD
(1881)

Did you know that the cartoon cat **Garfield** was (sort of) named after President Garfield? The cartoonist Jim Davis named the cat after his grandfather, James A. Garfield Davis, who had been named after President Garfield.

During the election of 1880, when Arthur ran as Garfield's vice president, he almost had to quit the race because he was born in Ireland. . . wasn't he?

21

CHESTER A. ARTHUR
(1881–1885)

OH NO HE WASN'T!

Arthur was born in Vermont, but during the campaign, his opponents spread rumors that he'd been born in Ireland, which would've disqualified him. Luckily, the lies didn't stick.

Our 22nd president was also POTUS number twenty-four! **Cleveland** ran for president three times, and won twice. Did you know that he was related to the person that Cleveland, Ohio, is named after?

23

22

Cleveland

GROVER CLEVELAND
(1885–1889; 1893–1897)

24

BENJAMIN HARRISON
(1889–1893)

Harrison was the grandson of William Henry Harrison. He was also one of the Founding Fathers who signed the Declaration of Independence. . . wasn't he?

OH NO HE WASN'T!

25

WILLIAM MCKINLEY
(1897–1901)

William McKinley was the third president to be assassinated.

The Declaration of Independence was signed in 1776, nearly 60 years before Benjamin was born. A different Benjamin Harrison (who happened to be his great-grandfather) *did* sign the declaration.

Did you know that after his death, McKinley's home state of Ohio made his favorite flower, the scarlet carnation, the official state flower?

Theodore Roosevelt loved the great outdoors. During his presidency he set up dozens of national forests and wildlife reserves. Roosevelt was such an animal lover that he happily gave permission for stuffed animal bears to be called "teddy bears" in his honor. . . didn't he?

OH NO HE DIDN'T!

THEODORE ROOSEVELT
(1901–1909)

26

Theodore Roosevelt hated the nickname "Teddy." He didn't give permission, but these cute toys were named after him anyway!

On a hunting trip, Roosevelt once refused to shoot an injured bear. The incident was made into a newspaper cartoon. A candy store owner saw it and displayed two stuffed animal bears in his store's window, calling them "Teddy bears" in honor of the president. Meanwhile, a New York toy store began selling German-made bear toys, which they also called "Teddy bears."

It's too bad that Theodore Roosevelt hated his nickname, because teddy bears are now loved by children around the world!

27

WILLIAM HOWARD TAFT
(1909–1913)

Did you know that our 27th president was the last one to have facial hair? The big beards and curly moustaches that many earlier presidents had ended with **Taft**. Maybe a hipster with a manicured moustache will become president one day and bring back the trend.

28

WOODROW WILSON
(1913–1921)

Woodrow Wilson saw America through World War I. **Did you know** that he was the last president to arrive at his inauguration in a horse-drawn buggy? The next president would show up in a car. Wilson also set up the White House screening room, where he'd watch the latest black-and-white movies.

29

Warren Harding was very popular. In fact, he was the first president to be supported by movie stars from Hollywood, which was a brand-new city back then.

WARREN G. HARDING
(1921–1923)

30

CALVIN COOLIDGE
(1923–1929)

Calvin Coolidge became president after Warren Harding died of a heart attack. Did you know that Coolidge is the only president born on the 4th of July? He also exercised by riding a mechanical horse named Thunderbolt.

Did you catch my T.V. debut?

31

Did you know that **Herbert Hoover** made history as the first person to be seen on a long-distance T.V. broadcast? He delivered a speech from Washington, D.C., to a laboratory in New York as part of a test.

Herbert Hoover also invented his own sport, called Hooverball! Two teams throw a big, heavy ball over a net, a bit like volleyball. It was hugely popular in the White House when Hoover was president.

HERBERT HOOVER
(1929–1933)

Franklin Roosevelt was the fifth cousin of Teddy Roosevelt. Nicknamed "FDR," he was one of the most important figures in American history. He led the country through the Great Depression, a time of great financial difficulty, and guided the nation during World War II. He was able to do all of this because he was elected four times! After his death, a constitutional amendment was passed to limit presidents to two terms.

FDR was permanently paralyzed from the waist down, which might have been linked with polio, although we're still not quite sure what caused it. He could walk short distances wearing leg braces and often used a wheelchair. Roosevelt kept his disability a secret from the public. . . didn't he?

OH NO HE DIDN'T!

32

FRANKLIN D. ROOSEVELT
(1933–1945)

Although Roosevelt didn't draw attention to his disability, and avoided being photographed in a wheelchair, his condition was well known for decades. FDR usually stood at public appearances, supported by an aide or his family. He even drove in a customized car operated by his hands instead of his feet!

Did you know that the "S" in **Harry S. Truman** doesn't stand for anything? It's not an initial or abbreviation—his middle name is just the letter "S"! It represents the names of both of his grandfathers: Anderson Shipp Truman and Solomon Young. That's why the "S" in his name is sometimes written without a period after it.

HARRY S. TRUMAN
(1945–1953)

CAMP DAVID

34

Coming in at number thirty-four is **Dwight David Eisenhower**, nicknamed "Ike." Did you know that he named the presidential holiday retreat in Maryland? He called it Camp David after his grandson.

DWIGHT D. EISENHOWER
(1953–1961)

President Kennedy is often known as JFK, though his friends and family called him Jack. JFK was one of our youngest presidents, and he was full of health and vigor. . . wasn't he?

OH NO HE WASN'T!

35

JOHN F. KENNEDY
(1961–1963)

Despite a public image of youthfulness, JFK almost died several times and suffered from constant back pain. Nevertheless, he proved himself as a war hero. Kennedy is the only president to be awarded the Purple Heart.

During World War II, Kennedy and his men were stranded on a Pacific island. While hiding from the enemy, the future president carved a message onto a coconut. Friendly civilians delivered it to U.S. forces, who sent a rescue party. President Kennedy made the coconut into a paperweight and kept it on his desk in the Oval Office!

Did you know that JFK was the last president to wear a hat at his inauguration? The tradition of wearing a hat began with the first president and ended with the 35th. By that time, people just didn't wear hats that much anymore.

36

Lyndon Johnson became president after JFK was assassinated, then was reelected in 1964 in a huge landslide victory. There were only six states that he didn't win!

Did you know that President Johnson was once a school teacher? He worked at a low-income, segregated Mexican American school in Texas for a year. His experiences inspired him to pass laws that helped oppressed people in many ways, including providing better education, healthcare, and cleaner environments.

LYNDON B. JOHNSON
(1963–1969)

This notorious president was forced out of office after being impeached. . . wasn't he?

OH NO HE WASN'T!

37

I QUIT!

RICHARD NIXON
(1969–1974)

Congress was about to vote on impeaching Nixon because of illegal acts he and his staff committed in a scandal called Watergate. But before anyone had a chance to vote, Nixon resigned. So he wasn't impeached, and he wasn't forced out of office. However, he is the first president ever to quit!

38

GERALD FORD
(1974–1977)

Nixon's vice president, **Gerald Ford**, took office after he quit. Did you know that Gerald Ford once worked as a model? He posed in his navy uniform for the cover of Cosmopolitan magazine in 1942 with his girlfriend, Phyllis Brown. Decades later, he even appeared in an episode of the popular soap opera *Dynasty*, playing himself.

39

JIMMY CARTER
(1977–1981)

This POTUS is best known today as a humanitarian. He grew up very poor and later in life spent a lot of time building homes in oppressed communities. Did you know that **President Carter** installed the first solar panels in the White House, all the way back in 1979?

40

Our 40th president was an actor and then governor of California before becoming POTUS. Did you know that **Ronald Reagan's** favorite snack was jelly beans? A candy company kept the White House supplied with jelly beans for all eight years of Reagan's presidency!

RONALD REAGAN
(1981–1989)

GEORGE H. W. BUSH
(1989–1993)

This president is famous for not liking broccoli. In fact, he disliked it so much that he banned the vegetable from being served at the White House. . . didn't he?

OH NO HE DIDN'T!

Although President Bush made it clear he didn't like broccoli, he never banned it. He knew the vegetable was healthy and kept it on the menu for anyone who wanted a helping.

So don't get any ideas! You always have to finish the vegetables on your plate, even if you become POTUS.

42

BILL CLINTON
(1993–2001)

Did you know that **Bill Clinton** is a talented saxophone player? He was the lead saxophonist in a prestigious band of young musicians from his home state of Arkansas. Clinton once performed in front of a live audience and millions of T.V. viewers on *The Arsenio Hall Show*, a popular T.V. talk show!

43

GEORGE W. BUSH
(2001–2009)

George W. Bush is the son of the 41st president, George H. W. Bush. The "W" in both of their names stands for "Walker," after their ancestor, George Walker. **Did you know** that president Bush took up portrait painting after leaving the White House? His second book of paintings featured portraits of people who have immigrated to the United States.

44

Our 44th president is the first African American president, as well as the first president who was born in Hawai'i. Did you know that **Barack Obama** is one of just eight presidents who were left-handed? The others are James A. Garfield, Herbert Hoover, Harry S. Truman, Gerald Ford, Ronald Reagan, George H. W. Bush, and Bill Clinton.

BARACK OBAMA
(2009–2017)

Like Ronald Reagan, this **POTUS** had a career in show business before going into politics. He appeared in many T.V. shows and movies, usually playing himself. He also produced and hosted a popular reality T.V. series.

DONALD TRUMP
(2017–2021)

Did you know that **Joe Biden** used to stutter when he was young? He worked hard to lessen the stutter by reciting poetry to himself in his bedroom mirror as a child, and he kept pushing to get better and better. His determination paid off, and Biden went on to become president of his senior class, and eventually President of the United States!

JOE BIDEN
(2021–PRESENT)

VICE PRESIDENTS

Every president has their veep, or vice president. The vice president has one main function: to step in for the president. . . don't they?

Step in for me. I'm double booked!

OH NO THEY DON'T!

It's true that the vice president is the president's backup, but this is only one of their many roles.

The veep also presides over the Senate, one of the two law-making bodies that make up Congress. Did you know that the vice president casts the deciding vote when there's a tie in the Senate?

If the president can no longer serve, the vice president is next in line, but it's not a done deal. Every veep must first be sworn in before they officially take over the new job.

HELP WANTED: VICE PRESIDENT

We always have a president and a vice president leading the United States. . . don't we?

OH NO WE DON'T!

Oh, the rejection. . .

DECLINED

There have been sixteen times when the United States VP spot has been vacant!

Sometimes it was because the VP had died or resigned, and sometimes it was after the VP took over for the president and a new one hadn't been appointed yet. Long ago, a high-ranking member of Congress became acting vice president if the position was open. These days, the president chooses a new VP who must be confirmed by Congress.

RIP

Did you know that seven vice presidents have died in office? Poor James Madison had two of his VPs die!

GEORGE CLINTON,
VP FOR JAMES MADISON
(MARCH 1809 – APRIL 1812)

ELBRIDGE GERRY,
VP FOR JAMES MADISON
(FROM 1813 – NOVEMBER 1814)

WILLIAM RUFUS DE VANE KING,
VP FOR FRANKLIN PIERCE
(FOR 6 WEEKS IN 1853)

HENRY WILSON,
VP FOR ULYSSES S. GRANT
(FROM MARCH 1873 –
NOVEMBER 1875)

THOMAS HENDRICKS,
VP FOR GROVER CLEVELAND
(FROM MARCH – NOVEMBER 1885)

GARRET HOBART,
VP FOR WILLIAM MCKINLEY
(FROM MARCH 1897 –
NOVEMBER 1899)

JAMES SHERMAN,
VP FOR WILLIAM HOWARD TAFT
(FROM MARCH 1909 –
OCTOBER 1912)

George Clinton is one of only two people to serve as veep for two presidents: once for **Thomas Jefferson** and again under **James Madison.**

Two vice presidents have resigned: **John C. Calhoun** (while serving as VP for Andrew Jackson) and **Spiro Agnew** (VP for Richard Nixon).

TAKING OVER

A total of fifteen veeps have become **POTUS**. Some of them succeeded a president who didn't finish their term, while others ran for president and won! But serving as VP doesn't make you a shoo-in—out of nineteen veeps who have run for president, only six have won!

Martin Van Buren, VP for Andrew Jackson, elected

John Adams, VP for George Washington, elected

Thomas Jefferson, VP for John Adams, elected

Chester A. Arthur, VP for James A. Garfield, succeeded

John Tyler, VP for William Henry Harrison, succeeded

Millard Fillmore, VP for Zachary Taylor, succeeded

Andrew Johnson, VP for Abraham Lincoln, succeeded

Theodore Roosevelt, VP for William McKinley, succeeded

Calvin Coolidge, VP for Warren G. Harding, succeeded

Harry S. Truman, VP for Franklin D. Roosevelt, succeeded

Lyndon B. Johnson, VP for John F. Kennedy, succeeded

Richard Nixon, VP for Dwight D. Eisenhower, elected

George H. W. Bush, VP for Ronald Reagan, elected

Joe Biden, VP for Barack Obama, elected

RUNNING MATES

The person running for president has always selected their vice-presidential running mate. . . haven't they?

OH NO THEY HAVEN'T!

Today, a person running for president selects the person they want to be VP, then they run together as a package deal.

But until 1800, the person who finished second in the presidential race became vice president! This system meant that the first two presidents were stuck with their main election opponents, who often disagreed with their policies. Those presidents and their VPs could best be described as frenemies.

WHEN VPs GO BAD

Speaking of frenemies, Aaron Burr, the vice president for Thomas Jefferson, shot a man during a duel. . . didn't he?

OH YES HE DID!

Aaron Burr shot and killed Alexander Hamilton, after what began as political disagreements became very personal.

As was the custom at the time, they agreed to settle their differences with a duel! Burr was never tried for killing Hamilton, but his reputation has been tarnished ever since.

HOME SWEET HOME

Vice presidents and their families live in the White House with the presidential family. . . don't they?

OH NO THEY DON'T!

In fact, they never have.

Today the vice president lives at a residence called the Naval Observatory, located at Number One Observatory Circle in Washington, D.C. The house is on the grounds of the U.S. Naval Observatory, where astronomers have studied the speed of light, quasars, eclipses, and many other things that are literally out of this world!

Before the Naval Observatory became the veep's official residence, the newly-elected vice president and their family had to find their own accommodation! Walter Mondale, vice president for Jimmy Carter, was the first VP to live at the Naval Observatory.

SWEARING IN

Before a veep can move into the Naval Observatory—and before they're officially the vice president—they must be sworn in. During the swearing-in ceremony, the newly-elected veep takes an oath to protect the Constitution. The ceremony always takes place in Washington, D.C.. . . doesn't it?

OH NO IT DOESN'T!

A few early VPs had their swearing-in ceremonies in New York or Philadelphia.

William King, Franklin Pierce's VP, was sworn in from Cuba! King suffered from an illness called tuberculosis and was in Cuba for treatment. He passed away shortly after returning to U.S. soil, serving only 45 days. He remains the only VP to be sworn in outside the United States.

Today, the vice president's swearing-in ceremony usually takes place on a specially constructed platform outside the Capitol building. This happens every four years on the 20th of January, also called Inauguration Day, when both the newly elected President and Vice President officially begin their terms.

A JOB FOR LIFE?

Just like the president, any vice president's career is limited to two four-year terms. . . isn't it?

OH NO IT ISN'T!

Although presidents are now limited to two terms in office, there is no term limit for vice presidents. If the American people kept electing you, you could be vice president forever!

VICE-PRESIDENTIAL FIRSTS

Did you know that **Kamala Harris**, vice president for Joe Biden, is the first female vice president? Two other women, Geraldine Ferraro and Sarah Palin, ran for veep but didn't win. Harris is also the first African American and the first Asian American VP!

The first Native American vice president was **Charles Curtis**, who served under Herbert Hoover. He was an enrolled member of the Kaw Nation.

CHARLES CURTIS
(1929–1933)

KAMALA HARRIS
(2021–)

44

MAKING HIS MARK

Al Gore, who was Bill Clinton's VP, invented the Internet. . . didn't he?

OH NO HE DIDN'T!

The veep didn't create the Internet himself, but he was key to promoting legislation, funding, and awareness to make it happen.

In 2005, **Al Gore** was presented with a Lifetime Achievement Award by the International Academy of Digital Arts and Sciences for his contributions to the development of the Internet.

VICE PRESIDENT TRIVIA

I'm telling you, it's empty like a coconut down there!

Did you know that two American cities were named after vice presidents? Dallas, Texas, was named after George Dallas, VP for James K. Polk, and Fairbanks, Alaska, was named after Charles Fairbanks, Theodore Roosevelt's VP.

Did you know that Richard Mentor Johnson, Martin Van Buren's veep, believed Earth was hollow? He asked Congress to fund a journey to the center of the planet! It was a hard pass for both the Senate and the House of Representatives.

Did you know that the term "veep" was created by a ten-year-old boy? Alben W. Barkley was Harry Truman's VP. His grandson Stephen came up with this nickname for him, which was picked up by the press and has been used ever since.

FIRST LADIES

Martha Washington, the wife of George Washington, was the first "First Lady" of the United States. . . wasn't she?

> **OH NO SHE WASN'T!**

> No matter how you address me, I'm still number one!

MARTHA WASHINGTON

This title didn't exist in the early days of our country's history.

People usually called **Martha Washington** "Lady Washington." First ladies after her were called "Mrs. President" or "Mrs. Presidentress."

HELPING OUT

> First first lady—and best niece ever.

Did you know that the first person to be referred to as "first lady" wasn't even the wife of a president? James Buchanan never married, so his first lady was his niece, **Harriet Lane**, who served as the White House hostess.

She wasn't the only first lady that wasn't married to the president. Andrew Jackson and Martin Van Buren asked their niece and daughter-in-law respectively to act as first lady. Chester A. Arthur and Grover Cleveland's first ladies were their sisters.

Thomas Jefferson's wife died before he became president, so two of his daughters took on the role. **Dolley Madison**, the wife of his secretary of state, James Madison, also helped out occasionally. She became the "official" first lady when her husband was elected to succeed Jefferson.

TAKE TWO

Did you know that two presidents had two first ladies?

Both John Tyler and Woodrow Wilson remarried after their first wives died while they were serving as president. After John Tyler's first wife, **Letitia Christian**, died he married **Julia Gardiner**. A year after **Ellen Axson**, passed away, Woodrow Wilson married **Edith Bolling Galt**.

FLOTUS

Today the First Lady of the United States is often referred to by the abbreviation FLOTUS. This term was first used for Ronald Reagan's wife, Nancy. When we elect a president with a husband instead of a wife, the husband will probably be known as the first gentleman and. . . FGOTUS?

Try saying that three times fast—or just once!

A BIG JOB

The First Lady of the United States isn't an elected position. Because of this, most first ladies didn't do much at all. . . did they?

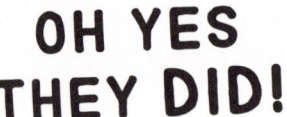

OH YES THEY DID!

Although the first lady has no official duties, most hosted people and events at the White House, devoted a lot of time to charity work, and attended official functions with—or sometimes in the place of—the president.

Many first ladies are well-known because of their many accomplishments, both during and outside their time as first lady! **Betty Ford** was the founder of the Betty Ford Center, a prestigious medical clinic that treats addiction. She was also a passionate supporter of women's rights and raised awareness and money to fight arthritis, HIV/AIDS, and breast cancer.

Lou Hoover, wife of Herbert Hoover, promoted physical fitness for girls. She was the national president of the Girl Scouts—twice! **Did you know** that the Girl Scouts began selling commercially baked cookies during her time as their president?

FOLLOWING THEIR OWN PATH

Because the role of first lady is so demanding, they all quit their jobs when they moved to the White House. . . didn't they?

OH NO THEY DIDN'T!

Most FLOTUSes did quit their jobs when they assumed the role, but there's no rule that says they had to.

Did you know that **Abigail Fillmore**, wife of Millard Fillmore, was the first first lady to keep her job after getting married? Back then, most women stopped working after marriage, but Abigail Fillmore continued teaching.

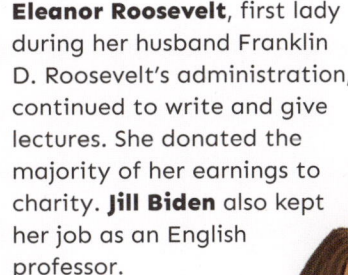

Eleanor Roosevelt, first lady during her husband Franklin D. Roosevelt's administration, continued to write and give lectures. She donated the majority of her earnings to charity. **Jill Biden** also kept her job as an English professor.

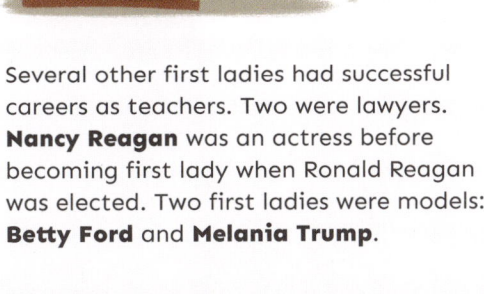

Several other first ladies had successful careers as teachers. Two were lawyers. **Nancy Reagan** was an actress before becoming first lady when Ronald Reagan was elected. Two first ladies were models: **Betty Ford** and **Melania Trump**.

WHITE HOUSE HOBBIES

When first ladies aren't hosting events or attending official functions, they spend time supporting charitable causes. First ladies have never had time to pursue any of their own interests. . . have they?

OH YES THEY HAVE!

In addition to fulfilling all of their responsibilities, many first ladies made time to pursue their hobbies.

Louisa Adams, first lady for John Quincy Adams, had many. She wrote plays, played the harp, and raised silkworms for fun!

Julia Tyler, wife of John Tyler, loved dancing and introduced a folk dance called the polka from Central Europe to the White House.

Today, a first lady's job is bigger than ever, but they have help at the White House. Their staff includes a social secretary who plans events, a press secretary who talks to the media, a floral designer responsible for the flower arrangements, and a chief of staff who looks after all their employees.

AMERICAN FIRST LADIES

All first ladies born after the Revolutionary War were born in the United States and had U.S. citizenship. . . didn't they?

OH NO THEY DIDN'T!

Melania Trump and **Louisa Adams** were both born outside the U.S. **Melania Trump** was born in what is now Slovenia and became a U.S. citizen at 36 years of age. **Louisa Adams**, wife of John Quincy Adams, was born in London. When her father became a U.S. citizen in 1776, she became one, too.

FIRST LADY TRIVIA

Did you know that **Eleanor Roosevelt** was the first first lady to fly in an airplane? The pilot of the plane was none other than the famous flier Amelia Earhart!

Shall we take to the skies, Amelia?

Edith Wilson, one of Woodrow Wilson's first ladies, had Native American ancestry. She was related to Pocahontas!

Michelle Obama is the first African American first lady, and she is known for her support of education for women and girls.

PRESIDENTIAL PETS

The presidents and their families all kept cats or dogs at the White House. . . didn't they?

OH NO THEY DIDN'T!

Most presidents had family pets, but many different kinds of animals called the White House home.

Cats and dogs were the most popular, followed by birds, horses, donkeys, reptiles, and rabbits. There were also rodents such as mice, hamsters, and guinea pigs, and farm animals like sheep, goats, and cows.

Some presidents received wild animals as gifts, which were then sent to zoos. Thomas Jefferson was gifted two grizzly bear cubs, while Theodore Roosevelt had a lion and a hyena! Calvin Coolidge was sent a bobcat, a tiger, lion cubs, a pygmy hippopotamus, a small antelope called a duiker, a wallaby, and a black bear.

Grover Cleveland's wife, Frances Cleveland, arrived at the White House with two dogs, five canaries, four cats, a baby deer, a cow, twelve white mice, two peacocks, two guinea pigs, two alligators, fish, and a large flock of chickens!

FAMOUS PETS

Some presidential pets have become famous. Bill Clinton's family pets had a book written about them, and so did George H. W. Bush's dog. President George W. Bush's two dogs stared in their own video series, and so did the Obamas' dogs. Fala, FDR's dog, appeared in two Hollywood films!

The Kennedys' dog Pushinka had a celebrity mom. Her mother, Strelka, was one of the first animals to go into space, spending a day in orbit aboard the spacecraft *Sputnik 5*.

Strelka

Fala

One giant leap for dogkind.

Pushinka

Dolley Madison's pet macaw Polly was feared by White House staffers. The parrot was free to roam the residence and often attacked people. One time, Polly bit President Madison's finger to the bone! Naughty birdie!

Only two presidents didn't have pets while in office: James K. Polk and Donald Trump. Although Andrew Johnson didn't have an official pet, he did take care of a family of mice that had made his bedroom their home. That counts as having pets, right?

PRESIDENTIAL TURKEYS

Every year before Thanksgiving, the president pardons a turkey, saving the bird from becoming dinner. Every president since George Washington participated in this age-old tradition. . . didn't they?

OH NO THEY DIDN'T!

Many presidents have been gifted turkeys for Thanksgiving.

Some ate the birds, while others didn't. The holiday custom of pardoning the turkey and letting them live was officially started in 1989 by President **George H.W. Bush.**

Many turkeys were sent to parks and farms after receiving their pardon. The turkeys pardoned between 2005 and 2009 lived their best lives at Disneyland or Disney World, where they served as honorary grand marshals for Disney's Thanksgiving Day Parade!

FIRST RACCOON?

Did you know that First Lady Grace Coolidge had a pet named Rebecca that she rescued from becoming Thanksgiving dinner? But Rebecca wasn't a turkey—she was a raccoon! Someone gave President Coolidge a raccoon for Thanksgiving, but the Coolidges had never eaten raccoon before, and didn't want to start. The furry critter became Grace Coolidge's pet instead.

I'm ready for some pumpkin pie.

For Christmas, Grace gave Rebecca a collar embroidered with the words "White House Raccoon." She walked her beloved pet on a leash around the White House grounds. Eggs were Rebecca's favorite food, and the raccoon was a keen participant in the 1927 Easter Egg Roll—no doubt for more eggs. Rebecca even had her own treehouse. The Coolidges were given another raccoon to be Rebecca's friend, but unfortunately, it ran away.

When the Coolidges left the White House, the Hoovers moved in. An opossum soon made Rebecca's treehouse his new home, and the Hoovers made him their pet. They named him Billy after President William Howard Taft, who was known as Billy to his friends.

MORE PRESIDENTIAL PETS

Here are even more presidential pets—and one famous vice-presidential pet. There are a lot of animals on these pages, but they still represent only a fraction of the numerous pets who have called the White House home!

JOE BIDEN Champ and Major (German Shepherds)

BARACK OBAMA Bo and Sunny (Portuguese Water Dogs)

GEORGE W. BUSH Miss Beazley and Barney (Scottish Terriers)

BILL CLINTON Socks (Cat) and **Buddy** (Labrador)

GEORGE H.W. BUSH Millie and Ranger (English Springer Spaniels)

Bill Clinton's Socks

RONALD REAGAN Lucky (Bouvier des Flandres) and **Rex** (Cavalier King Charles Spaniel)

JIMMY CARTER Grits (Border Collie), **Misty** (Siamese) and **Lewis Brown** (Afghan Hound)

GERALD FORD Liberty (Golden Retriever) and **Shan** (Cat)

RICHARD NIXON Checkers (Cocker Spaniel), **Pasha** (Yorkshire Terrier) and **King Timahoe** (Irish Setter)

John F. Kennedy's Charlie

LYNDON B. JOHNSON Him and Her (Beagles) and **Blanco** (Border Collie)

JOHN F. KENNEDY Debbie and Billie (Hamsters), **Tom Kitten** (A gray cat) **Robin** (Canary) and many more!

DWIGHT D. EISENHOWER Heidi (Weimaraner) and unnamed parakeet

HARRY S. TRUMAN Feller (Cocker Spaniel) and **Mike** (Irish Setter)

FRANKLIN D. ROOSEVELT Major (German Shepherd)

HERBERT HOOVER Two unnamed American alligators

CALVIN COOLIDGE Smoky (Bobcat)

WARREN HARDING Pete (Eastern gray squirrel)

WOODROW WILSON Old Ike (Shropshire ram)

Herbert Hoover's Unnamed alligators

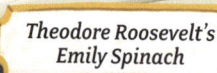

Theodore Roosevelt's Emily Spinach

WILLIAM TAFT **Pauline Wayne** (Holstein cow)

THEODORE ROOSEVELT **Emily Spinach** (Garter snake)

WILLIAM MCKINLEY **Washington Post** (Parrot)

BENJAMIN HARRISON **Mr. Reciprocity and Mr. Protection**
(Virginia opossums)

GROVER CLEVELAND Unnamed Japanese goldfish

CHESTER A. ARTHUR Unnamed bay horses

JAMES GARFIELD **Veto** (Newfoundland)

RUTHERFORD B. HAYES **Siam** (Siamese cat)

ULYSSES S. GRANT **Julia** (Horse)

ANDREW JOHNSON Unnamed family of white mice

ABRAHAM LINCOLN **Nanny and Nanko** (Goats)

JAMES BUCHANAN Two unnamed bald eagles

FRANKLIN PIERCE Unnamed Japanese Chin dogs

MILLARD FILLMORE **Mason and Dixon** (Ponies)

ZACHARY TAYLOR **Apollo** (Pony)

JOHN TYLER **Johnny Ty** (Canary)

WILLIAM HENRY HARRISON **Sukey** (Durham cow)

MARTIN VAN BUREN Two unnamed tiger cubs

ANDREW JACKSON **Poll** (African grey parrot)

JOHN QUINCY ADAMS Unnamed silkworms

JAMES MONROE **Buddy** (Spaniel)

JAMES MADISON **Polly** (Green macaw)

THOMAS JEFFERSON Two unnamed grizzly bear cubs

JOHN ADAMS **Cleopatra and Caesar** (Horses)

GEORGE WASHINGTON **Magnolia** (Arabian horse)

*Andrew Johnson's
Unnamed mice*

*Millard Fillmore's
Mason and Dixon*

*Thomas Jefferson's
Unnamed cubs*

*John Tyler's
Johnny Ty*

TIMELINE

Presidents and their vice presidents and first ladies.

1789-1797
George Washington

Martha Washington
VP: John Adams

1797-1801
John Adams

Abigail Adams
VP: Thomas Jefferson

1853-1857
Franklin Pierce

Jane Pierce
VP: William R. King

1850-1853
Millard Fillmore

Abigail Fillmore
VP: office vacant

1849-1850
Zachary Taylor

Margaret Taylor
Mary Elizabeth Bliss (Taylor's daughter) VP: Millard Fillmore

1845-1849
James K. Polk

Sarah Polk
VP: George M. Dallas

1857-1861
James Buchanan

Harriet Lane
(Johnson's niece)
VP: John C. Breckinridge

1861-1865
Abraham Lincoln

Mary Lincoln
VP: Hannibal Hamlin,
Andrew Johnson

1865-1869
Andrew Johnson

Eliza Johnson
VP: office vacant

1869-1877
Ulysses S. Grant

Julia Grant
VP: Schuyler Colfax,
Henry Wilson

1923-1929
Calvin Coolidge

Grace Coolidge
VP: Charles G. Dawes

1921-1923
Warren G. Harding

Florence Harding
VP: Calvin Coolidge

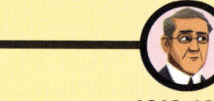

1913-1921
Woodrow Wilson

Ellen Wilson, Margaret Wilson
(Wilson's daughter) Helen Bones
(Wilson's cousin), Edith Wilson
VP: Thomas R. Marshall

1909-1913
William H. Taft

Helen Taft
VP: James S. Sherman

1929-1933
Herbert Hoover

Lou Hoover
VP: Charles Curtis

1933-1945
Franklin D. Roosevelt

Eleanor Roosevelt
VP: John N. Garner, Henry A.
Wallace, Harry S. Truman

1945-1953
Harry S. Truman

Elizabeth "Bess" Truman
VP: Alben W. Barkley

1953-1961
Dwight D. Eisenhower

Mary "Mamie" Eisenhower
VP: Richard M. Nixon

2021-
Joseph R. Biden

Jill Biden
VP: Kamala Harris

2017-2021
Donald J. Trump

Melania Trump
VP: Mike Pence

2009-2017
Barack Obama

Michelle Obama
VP: Joseph R. Biden

2001-2009
George W. Bush

Laura Bush
VP: Richard "Dick" Cheney

1801-1809
Thomas Jefferson

Martha Randolph and Mary Eppes
(Jefferson's daughters)
Dolley Madison (wife of the
Secretary of State)
VP: Aaron Burr, George Clinton

1809-1817
James Madison

Dolley Madison
VP: George Clinton,
Elbridge Gerry

1817-1825
James Monroe

Elizabeth Monroe
VP: Daniel D. Tompkins

1825-1829
John Quincy Adams

Louisa Adams
VP: John C. Calhoun

1841-1845
John Tyler

Letitia Tyler, Priscilla Tyler
(Tyler's daughter-in-law)
Julia Tyler VP: office vacant

1841
William Henry Harrison

Anna Harrison
VP: John Tyler

1837-1841
Martin Van Buren

Hannah Van Buren
VP: Richard M.
Johnson

1829-1837
Andrew Jackson

Emily Donelson (Jackson's niece)
Sarah Jackson, (Jackson's daughter
-in-law) VP: John C. Calhoun,
Martin Van Buren

1877-1881
Rutherford B. Hayes

Lucy Hayes
VP: William A. Wheeler

1881
James A. Garfield

Lucretia Garfield
VP: Chester A. Arthur

1881-1885
Chester A. Arthur

Mary McElroy
(Arthur's sister)
VP: office vacant

1885-1889
Grover Cleveland

Frances Cleveland
VP: Thomas A. Hendricks

1901-1909
Theodore Roosevelt

Edith Roosevelt
VP: Charles W. Fairbanks

1897-1901
William McKinley

Ida McKinley
VP: Garret A. Hobart,
Theodore Roosevelt

1893-1897
Grover Cleveland

Frances Cleveland
VP: Adlai E. Stevenson

1889-1893
Benjamin Harrison

Caroline Harrison, Mary McKee
(Harrison's daughter)
VP: Levi P. Morton

1961-1963
John F. Kennedy

Jacqueline Kennedy
VP: Lyndon B. Johnson

1963-1969
Lyndon B. Johnson

Claudia "Lady Bird" Johnson
VP: Hubert H. Humphrey

1969-1974
Richard M. Nixon

Thelma "Pat" Nixon
VP: Spiro T. Agnew,
Gerald Ford

1974-1977
Gerald Ford

Elizabeth "Betty" Ford
VP: Nelson Rockefeller

1993-2001
Bill Clinton

Hillary Clinton
VP: Albert "Al" Gore

1989-1993
George H. W. Bush

Barbara Bush
VP: Dan Quayle

1981-1989
Ronald Reagan

Nancy Reagan
VP: George H.W. Bush

1977-1981
Jimmy Carter

Rosalynn Carter
VP: Walter F. Mondale

MAP

The birthplace of every president

VIRGINIA

George Washington
Westmoreland County, Virginia

Thomas Jefferson
Shadwell, Virginia

James Madison
Port Conway, Virginia

James Monroe
Westmoreland County, Virginia

William Henry Harrison
Charles City County, Virginia

John Tyler
Charles City County, Virginia

Zachary Taylor
Orange County, Virginia

Woodrow Wilson
Staunton, Virginia

PENNSLYLVANIA

James Buchanan
Cove Gap, Pennsylvania

Joe Biden
Scranton, Pennsylvania

CALIFORNIA

Richard Nixon
Yorba Linda, California

Gerald Ford
Omaha, Nebras[ka]

OHIO

Ulysses S. Grant
Point Pleasant, Ohio

Rutherford B. Hayes
Delaware, Ohio

James A. Garfield
Moreland Hills, Ohio

Benjamin Harrison
North Bend, Ohio

William McKinley
Niles, Ohio

William Howard Taft
Cincinnati, Ohio

Warren G. Harding
Blooming Grove, Ohio

KENTUCKY

Abraham Lincoln
Hardin County
(now LaRue County),
Kentucky

Barack Obama
Honolulu, Hawai'i

MASSACHUSETTS

John Adams
Braintree (now Quincy), Massachusetts

John Quincy Adams
Braintree (now Quincy), Massachusetts

John F. Kennedy
Brookline, Massachusetts

George H. W. Bush
Milton, Massachusetts

VERMONT

Chester A. Arthur
Fairfield, Vermont

Calvin Coolidge
Plymouth, Vermont

Franklin Pierce
Hillsborough, New Hampshire

George W. Bush
New Haven, Connecticut

Grover Cleveland
Caldwell, New Jersey

NORTH CAROLINA

Andrew Johnson
Raleigh, North Carolina

James K. Polk
Mecklenburg County, North Carolina

Herbert Hoover
West Branch, Iowa

Ronald Reagan
Tampico, Illinois

Harry S. Truman
Lamar, Missouri

Bill Clinton
Hope, Arkansas

Jimmy Carter
Plains, Georgia

Andrew Jackson
Waxhaws region (border of North and South Carolina)

NEW YORK

Martin Van Buren
Kinderhook, New York

Millard Fillmore
Summerhill, New York

Theodore Roosevelt
New York City, New York

Franklin D. Roosevelt
Hyde Park, New York

Donald Trump
Queens, New York

TEXAS

Lyndon B. Johnson
Stonewall, Texas

Dwight D. Eisenhower
Denison, Texas

GLOSSARY

amendment A change or an addition to a document or set of rules; constitutional amendments are changes to the U.S. Constitution.

assassinate To kill an important person, such as a leader or a celebrity; four of our presidents were assassinated.

Bill of Rights A collection of rules made up of the first ten constitutional amendments that protect the freedoms of American citizens, including the freedom of speech and the right to a fair trial.

capital The city where the government of a country or state is based and where laws are passed.

Capitol The iconic domed building in Washington, D.C., where Congress meets.

citizen An official member of a country, state, or city; in the United States, you must be a U.S. citizen to vote and run for public office.

Civil War The struggle between the northern and southern states that took place from 1861–1865; slavery was abolished as a result of the war.

colony A settlement created by a government or group of people outside their own country, and usually far away; many parts of the United States were once colonies of Britain, Spain, or France.

Congress The part of our government that creates the laws; Congress is made up of the House of Representatives and the Senate.

constitution A set of rules that sets out what a government can and cannot do and protects the rights of citizens; the U.S. Constitution was written in 1787 to form the government of the newly created United States of America.

Declaration of Independence The document written in 1776 that proclaimed our independence from the British Empire.

duel A formal way of using weapons to settle disagreements, which was more common in the past and is illegal today because it often led to severe injuries and death.

Emancipation Proclamation A document created by President Lincoln during the Civil War, which declared all enslaved people in Confederate-controlled areas to be free.

executive order An order given by the president that the government must follow; executive orders that contradict the U.S. Constitution can be stopped by Congress and the courts.

first lady The wife, female partner, or chosen individual who fulfils public duties to assist the President.

FLOTUS An abbreviation of the title First Lady of the United States.

Founding Fathers The group of leaders who created the United States of America; this term includes men who held commanding roles in the Revolutionary War and drafted the Declaration of Independence and the U.S. Constitution.

host/hostess A person in charge of guests at an event; one of the first lady's traditional roles is to host guests at the White House.

House of Representatives One of the two parts of the U.S. Congress, whose members are each elected to two-year terms to represent a different region; states with larger populations have more representatives.

humanitarian A person who uses words or actions to help people in need, especially during crises and conflicts; their efforts can include donating money to a cause, giving their time, passing compassionate laws, or creating charitable organizations.

impeach To accuse a high-ranking government official of breaking the law; the House of Representatives can vote to charge the president of wrongdoing and force them to stand trial in the Senate.

inauguration The event that marks the beginning of an elected official's term; a presidential inauguration involves a swearing-in ceremony in which the new president promises to take on their duties and responsibilities for the people.

legislation The process of creating and passing laws; in the U.S. government, Congress comes up with proposals called bills for new laws.

Naval Observatory The name of the home where the vice president and their family live; its official name is Number One Observatory Circle.

pardon An order by the president that forgives a person for a crime.

POTUS An abbreviation for the title President of the United States.

president The elected official who runs the executive branch of government and also represents our country on the world's stage.

Revolutionary War The conflict that won our country's independence from the British Empire.

running mate A person selected by a candidate to be their partner and run as a package deal; the term is most commonly used for a

presidential candidate's choice of a vice-presidential candidate.

Senate One of the two parts of the U.S. Congress, consisting of two elected senators from each state, who serve six-year terms.

stutter A speech impediment in which a person can't help repeating sounds or words, or has trouble getting particular words or sounds out.

succeed To take over as the next person in office, such as when a vice president becomes president in the place of someone who has died.

term The amount of time that someone is allowed to serve in an elected office; for example, a president serves a four-year term.

veep A shortened version of the title vice president.

vice president An elected official who serves our country to support and advise the president.

War of 1812 An armed conflict fought between the United States and Great Britain from 1812–1815 due to disagreements on a wide range of issues, from trade to territory and the treatment of sailors serving on American ships.

White House The building where the president and their family live and work, located at 1600 Pennsylvania Avenue in Washington, D.C..

World War I A war fought from 1914–1918, which involved many of the world's powers; the war resulted in huge numbers of casualties as well as instability that would eventually lead to another world war.

World War II A global conflict lasting from 1939–1945, which pitted the Axis powers (Germany, Japan, Italy, and their allies) against the Allies (including the United States, United Kingdom, Soviet Union, and China); it was the deadliest war in history.

ABOUT THE AUTHOR

Eric Huang was born in New Jersey and grew up in California. He loved mythology, nature, comic books, and more than anything else. . . dinosaurs. When Eric went to college he studied paleontology, hoping to find fossils. But life took him all the way to Australia, where he found kangaroos and koalas instead. Since then, Eric has worked with Disney, Penguin Books, and LEGO—and found a few fossils along the way. He now teaches at City, University of London, writes books, and makes podcasts.

Acknowledgements

Thank you to Holly, Alice, and Nancy for all of your invaluable feedback. Thank you Shannon for signing up this series. And thanks to Angela, Brian, Elias, Emma, Nic, and my mom for pushing me to write!

Eric Huang

ABOUT THE ILLUSTRATOR

Sam Caldwell is an illustrator based in Glasgow where he lives with his wife and two cats: Tonks and Luna. Sam loves inventing characters and creating images packed full of detail, texture, and color. He is passionate about animals and nature, and when he's not drawing, Sam can often be found exploring the Scottish Highlands. He has illustrated many books for children, including the award winning *Do Bears Poop In The Woods*?

Acknowledgements

A big thanks to Kat and Susi for all of the fantastic design work and steering of the ship on this series. Thank you also Doreen, Kate and, Tom for the opportunity and continued support.

Sam Caldwell